© 2012 Age of Learning, Inc.
Published by Age of Learning, Inc., P.O. Box 10458, Glendale, California 91209.
No part of this work may be reproduced in whole or in part, or stored in a retrieval system,
or transmitted in any form or by any means, electronic, mechanical, photocopying,
recording, or otherwise, without written permission of the publisher.
ABCmouse.com and associated logos are trademarks and/or
registered trademarks of Age of Learning, Inc.

Library of Congress Cataloging-in-Publication Data
Ham with Jam?/Age of Learning, Inc.
Summary: In this Word Family Beginning Reader, Pam and Sam learn to like
something new by combining each other's favorite foods.

ISBN: 978-1-62116-009-0
Library of Congress Control Number: 2012912288

21 20 19 18 17 16 15 14 13 12   1 2 3 4 5
Printed in the U.S.A., on 10% recycled paper. ♻
First printing, October 2012

Age of Learning, Inc., Glendale, California

This book is also available at **ABCmouse.com**, the award-winning early learning online curriculum.

Find free apps at **ABCmouse.com/apps**.

Pam is a girl.

Pam likes jam.

Sam is a boy.

Sam likes ham.

One day Pam
said to Sam,
"Will you eat
some of my jam?"

Sam said he would not eat jam!

Pam said she would not eat ham!

"I have a plan,"
Pam said to Sam.
"Maybe jam tastes
good on ham!"

Pam took out
her jar of jam.

She put some on
a piece of ham.

"This is good,"
Pam said to Sam.
"Try a piece of
ham with jam."

Sam put jam on top of ham.

Then he ate his
piece of ham.

Sam told Pam,
"Now I like jam!"

And Pam told Sam,
"Now I like ham!"

The End